Here Comes Harley!

Harley Comes Home

Gina Fuscaldo Franco

Illustrated by Aleksandra Dragović

Outskirts Press, Inc.
http://www.outskirtspress.com

ISBN: 978-1-9772-2756-0

Illustrated by Aleksandra Dragovic © 2021 Gina Fuscaldo Franco

Outskirts Press and the "OP" logo are trademarks belonging to Outskirts Press, Inc.

PRINTED IN THE UNITED STATES OF AMERICA

A special Thank You
to my son, Michael,
for bringing Harley into our home
and our lives!

This book is dedicated to Mike's first dog, Cookie.
Once by our side forever in our hearts.

Harley has a
best friend.
His name is Mike.

Mike took Harley home.

Harley met
Grandma at home.

Grandma gave
Harley cookies.

And Grandma
took Harley for walks.

Harley liked
to read
with Grandma.

And Harley liked to exercise with Grandma!

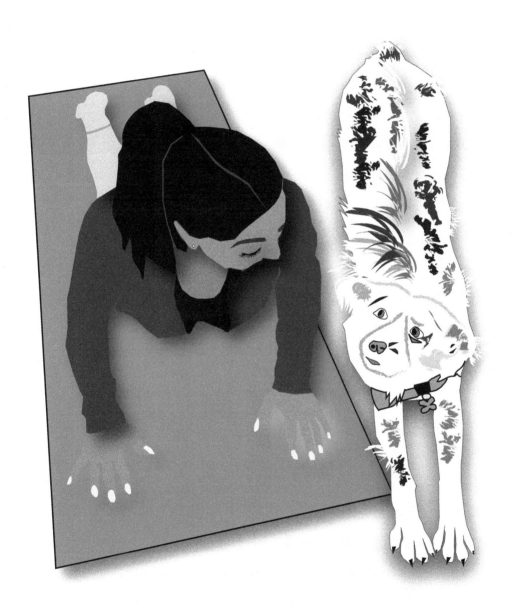

After dinner
Mike took Harley
out to play.

Harley waved
to Grandma.

Goodbye Grandma! See you later!

Harley
had fun
with Mike.

She chased
the ball and
she did tricks.

When Harley
came home,
she was tired!

Grandma was there
to tuck her in.

Goodnight Harley!
Goodnight Grandma!
Goodnight Mike!

And Harley fell asleep.

Harley liked
her new Home.

CPSIA information can be obtained
at www.ICGtesting.com
Printed in the USA
BVHW052332041021
618137BV00001B/2